Contents

Written by
Julia Golding

Illustrated by
Sonia Possentini

Series editor **Dee Reid**

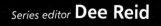

Before reading *Second Chance*

Characters

Gideon

Taylor

Crystal

Tricky words

ch1 p5 disguised
ch2 p8 balcony
ch2 p10 gleaming
ch2 p11 choking

ch3 p14 paramedic
ch4 p18 gaze
ch4 p19 frantic

Introduction

Gideon is a dark angel. He was kicked out of heaven for breaking the rules. Now he tries to use his powers as an angel to help people on earth. If he can do enough good on earth he might be allowed back to heaven. One day Gideon meets Taylor who has run away from home. Something terrifying is about to happen to her.

Second
Chance

Chapter One

My name is Gideon. I am a dark angel.
I was kicked out of heaven for breaking
the rules. Now I spend my time trying to help
humans make the right choice when they reach a
crossroads in their short lives. But some humans
can be hard to help.

One day, I met Taylor. She had left home after an argument with her mum and her step-dad. She was angry with them and she had decided not to go back home. I saw her sitting on her own in the shopping centre. She looked really miserable.

Then an angel messenger came. I knew her from
when I used to be in heaven. Crystal is a beautiful
angel, with white wings, dark skin like mine, and
long dark hair. But she had disguised herself
as a bag lady, and she used an old coat to hide
her light.

She sat down next to Taylor, delivered her
message, then picked up her bags and left.

I stopped Crystal before she returned to heaven and asked how the meeting with Taylor had gone. At first she didn't want to talk to me, as she knows I'm a fallen angel, but then she changed her mind.

"The meeting didn't go well," said Crystal. "Taylor wasn't ready to listen and I know something really bad is going to happen if she stays here. See if you can help her. Maybe this is your chance to set things right."

She gave me a gentle smile and then took off her old coat, spread her wings and flew off into the sunset. I miss my wings, now I only have scars where my wings used to be. But most of all I miss my friends in heaven.

Chapter Two

So I stayed and watched the girl. It got dark and the lights in the shopping centre went off, leaving only the window displays lit. Taylor hid in the shadows as the guard made his rounds. Neither of them saw me standing on the balcony above.

I may be a fallen angel but I can still get inside people's heads and read their thoughts. I could feel Taylor's unhappiness. She thought that no one loved her and she wanted to make her mum sorry. She wanted her step-dad, his stupid daughter and his screaming toddler to push off so that she and her mum could have their old lives back.

Then a man came out of the shadows in the shopping centre. His hood was up so that only two gleaming eyes could be seen in the depths. I sensed the desperate greed that drove him to steal to get his next drug fix. A girl on her own like Taylor made an easy target.

Even before he saw her I began running, wishing I still had my wings.

The man sprang on Taylor and drew a knife.

"Hand over your bag," he shouted.

Taylor gave a yelp of terror. She clutched

her bag closer to her chest. The man waved the blade

in her face. "Give it to me."

"It's all I've got," said Taylor, terror choking her. I ran

to help as they fought over the bag. I saw the knife

raised high to slash at Taylor's face.

I dived and landed between Taylor and the blade. I felt pain shoot through me as the knife struck. Angels have many powers but if we are attacked we get hurt. I had never before heard of an angel being stabbed. I wondered if I was about to be the first angel to discover what happened to us if we died.

Chapter Three

The next thing I knew I was being taken into the hospital. Someone was holding my hand. It was Taylor and she was crying.

"They've got the guy who did this to you. You'll be OK," she promised me.

I wasn't sure of that. Angels can sense the strength of the life in people and my strength was fading fast like a candle burning down.

The paramedic was talking to a doctor. "We can't get any readings from him – no heart beat, no pulse. And look at his back! He has strange marks on him. I don't know if they are scars or a tattoo. They look almost like wings to me but they can't be. I've never seen anything like it."

The doctor put her fingers to my neck to see if she could feel a pulse, then she saw me watching her.

"He would seem to be alive even if he has no heart beat and no pulse," she said.

Then she turned to Taylor. "What's his name?" she asked.

Taylor shrugged. "I don't know," she said. "I've never seen him before but he just saved my life."

"Is there someone we can call for you?" the doctor asked Taylor.

"It's OK," said Taylor. "I've just sent my mum a message to tell her where I am."

When I heard Taylor say that, I felt the pain in my side begin to ease.

"We'll stitch up his wound," said the doctor. "Go to the waiting room. We'll give you a shout if there's any news."

Chapter Four

I was taken into a treatment room. I saw
Taylor looking through the curtains before the
nurses drew them shut. She was willing me to
live just as I was willing her to go home.

The nurse injected me with something to ease the
pain but it didn't work on me. The stitches melted
in my flesh before they could close the wound.

Then the doctor went to get her boss to see if he had any ideas on how to treat this strange man. I knew I had to leave before they realised I wasn't human. Only time could heal me, not their medicine. Taylor slipped through the curtains and took my hand.

"You shouldn't be in here," I said. "You should go home."

Taylor nodded. She looked up and I followed her gaze. Taylor's mum was standing in the corridor. She had tears running down her face.

"Take your second chance," I whispered to Taylor.

"Mum!" cried Taylor, throwing herself into her mum's arms.

"I'm sorry I said all those things," said Taylor's mum. "I have been frantic with worry! Remember, I love you so much. Come home with me now. Jeff, Kelsie and Tommy are waiting for us. Just give us all a chance to be a family. It is going to be OK."

She put her arm around Taylor and they turned to go. It was time for me to go too. I was weak but I could still make myself unseen. I melted into the shadows. Maybe Crystal was right. If I do enough good things on earth I might get the chance to return to heaven.

Quiz

Text comprehension

Literal comprehension
p4 Why had Taylor left home?

p12 What did Gideon do as the man attempted to stab Taylor?

p15 Why was the doctor puzzled when she examined Gideon?

Inferential comprehension
p15–16 Why does the pain in Gideon's side begin to ease?

p18 Why is Taylor's mum crying?

p20 Why might Crystal be right?

Personal response
- If you were Taylor, who would you think Gideon was?
- What would you be thinking if you were the doctor examining Gideon?
- Do you think Gideon was a good guardian angel to Taylor? Why?

Author's style

p14 What simile does the author use to describe how Gideon's strength was fading?

p18 Why does the author describe Gideon as a 'strange man'?

p18 Why is 'slipped' a good verb to use to describe how Taylor came back to speak to Gideon?

Characters

- **Mum**
- Taylor
- **Jeff** (Taylor's step-dad)
- **Grandad**

Setting the scene

Taylor's mum has recently remarried. Taylor doesn't get on very well with her step-dad, Jeff. She resents the fact that she has to share a bedroom with Jeff's little boy, Tommy, while Kelsie, Jeff's daughter, has a room to herself.

Mum: Taylor, get back in here! I'm talking to you!

Taylor: You always do the talking, but you never listen! You don't care what I think!

Jeff: Don't speak to your mother like that.

Taylor: You let Kelsie have her own bedroom and I have to share with the toddler from hell!

Jeff: And don't talk about your little step-brother like that. Tommy is just lively – like all three year olds.

Taylor: He has torn all my posters and scribbled in my school books. He isn't lively. He's a menace!

Grandad: When I was young, children wouldn't dare give their parents such cheek. Your mum and step-dad do their best for you, Taylor.

Taylor: Really? Since mum married Jeff, I might as well not exist. All that matters to mum now is Jeff, Kelsie and Terrible Tommy.

Mum: That's not true, Taylor. We just need time to get used to living as a family. Having a toddler around is hard work for all of us.

Grandad: When I was young, we were seen and not heard.

Taylor: Well I feel like the invisible girl – not seen *and* not heard.

Jeff: You are not the only person in this family, young lady.

Taylor: I just want things to be fair. Kelsie is only a year older than me. Why do I have to share with a toddler when she gets her own room?

Mum: Kelsie is studying for her exams. She needs somewhere quiet to do her homework.

Taylor: And you think I don't need somewhere quiet to do my homework?

Jeff: Well, we don't see you doing much homework, do we?

Grandad: When I was your age, I did three hours each night during the week and more at the weekend.

Taylor: You did not, Grandad. You always
told me you went out playing football
whenever you got the chance.

Mum: What your Grandad did or did not do is
not the point. Kelsie needs to pass her
exams. She wants to be a doctor. Her
exams will be over in a few months.

Taylor: Then what? After I've had a few months
of Tommy scribbling all over my books
and jumping on me every morning, then
Kelsie and I swap so I get the room and
she shares with Tommy?

Mum: Well…

Jeff: Your mum and I have talked this over.

Mum: After these exams, Kelsie will be
studying for her AS exams.

Jeff: And then she has her A Levels.

Taylor: See what I mean? It's all about Kelsie. Kelsie keeps the bedroom because she is the favourite and I get nothing.

Jeff: Families have to learn how to live together.

Taylor: I don't see anyone else offering to sleep in the same room as Tommy.

Grandad: You don't expect me to give up my room at my age, do you?

Taylor: Whatever. I'm out of here.

Mum: Where are you going?

Taylor: Just out.

Jeff: What do you mean 'just out'?

Grandad: You need to let us know where you are going.

Taylor: As if anyone in this house cares about me.

Jeff: We all care about you.

Mum: When are you going to be back?

Taylor: Not until I can have my own room.

Jeff: But we've told you why you have to share with Tommy.

Taylor: No. You've told me why Kelsie and Tommy mean more to you than I do. You never listen to me. I'm out of here!

Quiz

Text comprehension

p23 What different attitudes to Tommy's behaviour do Jeff and Taylor have?

p23 How do you think Taylor feels when Grandad joins in the argument?

p25 Do you think it's fair that Taylor has to share a bedroom with Tommy? Why?

Vocabulary

p23 Find a word meaning 'nuisance'.

p24 Find a word meaning 'cannot be seen'.

p27 Find a word meaning 'preferred'.

Before reading The History of Angels

Find out about

• how angels have been presented in paintings, poems, sculpture and body art.

New vocabulary

p31 messengers
p31 communicate
p31 fascinated
p32 Middle Ages

p32 warriors
p32 protectors
p34 Victorian times

Introduction

Many religions describe messengers who communicate between gods and humans. These messengers are called angels. Hundreds of years ago, artists painted angels with wings and today that is the most popular image of an angel. Many people also think of angels as creatures who protect humans.

The History of Angels

In the holy books of many religions you can read about messengers who communicate between gods and humans. In the Christian religion these messengers are called angels. The Christian holy book, the Bible, describes angels with four or six wings. At first, artists painted angels without wings but, from the 4th century, they began painting angels with wings and people became fascinated with these winged messengers.

In the Middle Ages, popular scenes for artists to paint were scenes from the Bible. The Bible describes how the Angel Gabriel comes from heaven to tell Mary she is going to have a baby. The many paintings of this scene all show the Angel Gabriel as a man with big wings.

Not all paintings show angels as messengers. Some paintings show angels as warriors or protectors. The angel called Michael, who is in the holy books of many religions, is always painted as a strong warrior.

In the holy books, Michael is described fighting dragons. The holy books also describe Michael fighting Satan – and winning the fight! Many artists have created paintings showing Michael's fight with Satan.

This painting shows the angel Michael fighting Satan.

John Milton was a poet who lived in the 17th century. He wrote about bright angels who are on the side of good (like Michael in the holy books) and fallen angels who were thrown out of heaven for breaking the rules. The poet and artist, William Blake (1757–1827), painted angels as strong creatures who were protective of humans.

In Victorian times, people began to confuse the idea of angels with the idea of what happens to humans after they die. At that time many mothers and babies died in childbirth so many families had lost a baby brother, sister, or a mother. Children were often told that the baby or mother who had died had become an angel who would always guard them and protect them. These angels were called guardian angels.

Also at that time, artists changed their way of painting angels and began painting them as pretty women in long white dresses. This was a big change from the paintings that showed angels as strong and powerful and ready to fight dragons! Today you can still see these pretty angels on Christmas cards or at the top of Christmas trees.

Artists in the 20th century have gone back to the idea of angels as strong, powerful figures. This huge angel stands near the A1 in Gateshead. It is about as different from a Christmas tree angel as you can get!

The Angel of the North

The Angel of the North

What is it made of?	Steel
When was it made?	1994 – 1998
Who created it?	Anthony Gormley
How tall is it?	20 metres
How long are its wings?	54 metres
How much does it weigh?	200 tonnes

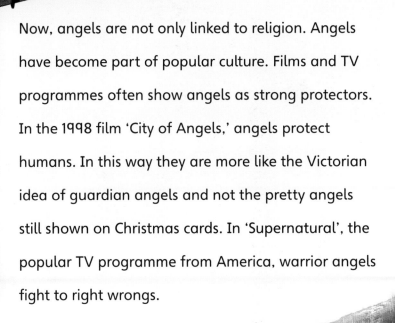

Now, angels are not only linked to religion. Angels have become part of popular culture. Films and TV programmes often show angels as strong protectors. In the 1998 film 'City of Angels,' angels protect humans. In this way they are more like the Victorian idea of guardian angels and not the pretty angels still shown on Christmas cards. In 'Supernatural', the popular TV programme from America, warrior angels fight to right wrongs.

Angels are one of the most popular subjects for body art. The actress, Gemma Arterton, has a tattoo of angel wings behind her ear, and David Beckham has a guardian angel tattooed on his back. Why do you think angels are so popular as a tattoo?

Quiz

Text comprehension

Literal comprehension

p32–33 What is the popular image of the angel called Michael?

p34 Why did the idea of guardian angels become popular in Victorian times?

p37 What is the 'Angel of the North' made of?

Inferential comprehension

p32 Why do you think angels are so popular in art?

p33 Why do you think Milton had bright and fallen angels in his poems?

p36–37 Why do you think Antony Gormley chose to create a sculpture of an angel?

Personal response

- Why do you think Victorian artists changed the way they painted angels?
- Would you like the idea of having a guardian angel?
- Do you think body art is attractive?

Non-fiction features

p31–36 Which words tell the reader the time sequence of events?

p34 In what ways does this image illustrate the text above it?

p38 Think of a subheading for this page.

Published by Pearson Education Limited, Edinburgh Gate, Harlow, Essex, CM20 2JE.

www.pearsonschoolsandfecolleges.co.uk

Text © Pearson Education Limited 2012

Edited by Jo Dilloway
Designed by Tony Richardson and Siu Hang Wong
Original illustrations © Pearson Education Limited 2012
Illustrated by Sonia Possentini
Cover design by Siu Hang Wong
Cover illustration © Pearson Education Limited 2012

The right of Julia Golding to be identified as author of this work has been asserted by her in
accordance with the Copyright, Designs and Patents Act 1988.

First published 2012

16 15 14 13 12
10 9 8 7 6 5 4 3 2 1

British Library Cataloguing in Publication Data
A catalogue record for this book is available from the British Library

ISBN 978 0 435 07157 8

Printed at Scotprint, UK.

Acknowledgements
The author and publisher would like to thank the following individuals and organisations for
permission to reproduce photographs:

(Key: b-bottom; c-centre; l-left; r-right; t-top)

Bridgeman Art Library Ltd: The Archangel Michael defeating Satan (oil on canvas), Reni, Guido
(1575-1642) / Private Collection 33; Corbis: Alfredo Dagli Orti / The Art Archive 32; Mary Evans
Picture Library: INTERFOTO / TV-yesterday 34, Retrograph Collection 35; Glow Images: 1, 31;
Getty Images: Film Magic / Jason LaVeris 38; Shutterstock.com: Joe Cox 36-37

Cover images: Back: Mary Evans Picture Library: Retrograph Collection

All other images © Pearson Education

Every effort has been made to contact copyright holders of material reproduced in this book. Any
omissions will be rectified in subsequent printings if notice is given to the publishers.